ANIMAL + RESCUE

The Lonely Kitten

ANIMAL MAGIC

This series is for my riding friend Shelley,
who cares about all animals.

STRIPES PUBLISHING
An imprint of the Little Tiger Group
1 Coda Studios, 189 Munster Road, London SW6 6AW

A paperback original
First published in Great Britain in 2008
This edition published in 2018

ISBN: 978-1-84715-925-0

ANIMAL RESCUE

The Lonely Kitten

TINA NOLAN

stripes

ANIMAL MAGIC
RESCUE CENTRE

🏠 **HOME**

🐾 **ADOPT**

✋ **FRIENDS**

MEET THE ANIMALS IN NEED OF A HOME!

BECKS

The sweetest, most affectionate girl ever! Please let her curl up on your lap.

SUZI

Suzi has just arrived. She needs a quiet home with no children and no other pets.

ROCKY

A beautiful boy who needs long walks and lots of love. Can you give him a home?

- 📰 NEWS
- ✋ HELP US
- 📞 CONTACT

 **£ DONATE!**

DOUGAL

Soft, cuddly and very patient, Dougal has the friendliest nature. But watch out – he's ticklish!

MAXWELL

Maxwell is a lovable, lively hamster, who'll make a great pet. You know you can't resist!

OLIVER

Oliver is 12 hands high and would suit a confident young rider. Could that be you?

Chapter One

"How do I look?" Eva Harrison asked her friend, Annie Brooks. She stood at Annie's door, wearing her new Animal Magic sweatshirt. It was bright red, with a small white-and-gold logo on the front.

"You look ... magic!" Annie grinned.

"They came in the post this morning," Eva explained. "It was Jen's idea – she had it after I'd been on the Tina O'Neill Show on TV. We've all got one!"

"Cool," Annie sighed.

"Dad says we're really popular at the moment and our website is getting loads more traffic than usual. We want to order more sweatshirts and sell them. It'll help raise money for the rescue centre. Hey, Holly, stay down!" Eva turned to her lively Border collie puppy, who was jumping up at Annie. "Oops!"

"Too late!" Annie glanced down at the muddy paw prints on her pink-and-white dressing gown. "Never mind – it'll wash off. How are you, Holly? Have you been on a nice walk?" She stroked the lively pup.

"Down by the river," Eva explained. "I'm doing obedience training with her, so we go out early every morning before school. Anyway, as today's Saturday and Mum says we'll be extra busy, I came to ask if you'd like to help out in Reception."

Annie's eyes lit up. "I'll be there in a flash," she promised. "Oh, and Eva…"

"Yep?" Already halfway down the Brookses' driveway, Eva paused.

"Order an Animal Magic sweatshirt for me. I'll pay with my pocket money."

"Sure thing," Eva replied, putting Holly on the lead and dashing off.

Animal Magic Rescue Centre stood next door to Annie's house on Main Street in Okeham village. It didn't take long for Eva to settle Holly down in the house and make her way across the yard to Reception, where she found the room already crowded with visitors.

"I read about Becks the Yorkshire terrier on your website," a woman was telling Heidi Harrison. "I'd like to offer her a home."

Eva's mum smiled brightly. She was wearing her red sweatshirt under her white vet's coat. "Can I take your name and a few other details? Becks is very popular – two possible owners have already visited her earlier this week."

"Here's Suzi." Jen, Heidi's assistant, was showing another woman a black cat who had come into the centre only the day before. "You can see how she's licked the fur off her tummy – that's over-grooming due to stress, I'm afraid."

"Poor thing!" the woman murmured. "Will the fur grow back eventually?"

"Oh yes – definitely," Jen assured her.

Quietly, Eva made her way behind the desk to find her brother, Karl, printing out an email.

"Take a look at this," he said, grinning.

Eva picked up the printout. "Dear Animal Magic," she read out loud, "Scott and I saw the New Year feature

ɔou on the Tina O'Neill Show
ve wanted to write and tell you
how Honey, our retriever, is getting
along. She's now fully grown and is
much loved, with a silky-soft golden
coat and gorgeous, dark brown eyes. She
loves her walks with Scott in the park
at the back of Beech Grove – all thanks
to you! With very best wishes, Ruth
Penny."

"What do you think of that?" Karl
asked.

"Cool." Eva blushed and looked
up from the email. She remembered
Honey so well – how she'd been
secretly dumped on their doorstep by
the Pennys' lodger, abandoned in a
cardboard box. She put the printout
down on the table. "Mum, what job

shall I do first?" she asked, breaking
into Heidi's conversation.

"Groom Dougal, please. His new owner
is coming to collect him at ten o'clock."

Eva nodded. "Will you ask Annie to
come to the kennels when she arrives?"

"Will do," Heidi replied.

Escaping from the busy Reception,
Eva picked up a dog comb and brush
from the storeroom and hurried on to
the kennels. "Hi, Becks, hi, Rocky!"
she greeted the yappy Yorkshire terrier
and a big, dark grey dog with floppy
ears and sad eyes. She went up to
Rocky's door. "Are you wondering how
come nobody wants to adopt you?"
she murmured. "Becks gets all the
attention, doesn't he? That's because
he's little and cute."

Rocky lowered his head and gave a short whine.

"I'm not saying you're not cute!" Eva insisted. "You are – you're totally beautiful. But not as many people want to give homes to dogs as big as you."

Rocky's long tail wagged slowly. He stared longingly at Eva.

Tearing herself away from him, Eva

went along the row of kennels until she came to Dougal.

The long-haired Labrador-cross came quietly to the door. All around, other dogs barked and yapped.

"OK, Dougal, it's your big day," Eva explained. She went in and began brushing the soft, cream hair on Dougal's chest. "We'll make you look your very best – yes, I know the brush tickles but you have to stand still and let me groom you!"

"Can I help?" Annie asked, pushing open the door to the kennel unit. She was dressed in jeans, wellies and a sky-blue padded jacket.

Eva nodded. "Dougal's ticklish. Can you hold his collar while I brush him?"

Together the two girls brushed out

every tangle as Dougal wriggled and sighed. When they had finished, he stood up and shook himself.

"You look gorgeous!" Annie laughed.

"I have to take him to Reception," Eva told her. "You can give Becks a quick brush if you like."

So Annie unlocked the Yorkie's kennel and began a pamper session. When Eva came back it was time to take Rocky for his walk.

"See how good he is on the lead." Eva led Rocky out of a side door and across the yard. She handed him to Annie and slipped into the house, coming back out with an excited Holly. "I thought Rocky might like some company!" she grinned.

They set off down the narrow footpath to the side of the rescue centre, letting the two dogs off the lead as soon as they reached the riverside. Rocky bounded ahead, with Holly scampering beside him. When they came to the old stone bridge they waited for Eva and Annie.

"Good dogs!" Eva told them. She patted them, then drew a ball out of her jacket pocket. "Watch this, Annie. I've taught Holly to fetch." She threw the ball back along the path.

Holly raced after it and brought it back.

"Woof!" Rocky's deep bark begged the girls to throw again.

This time Annie threw and it was Rocky who grabbed the ball.

"Rocky's gorgeous. How come he ended up at Animal Magic?" she asked.

Eva shrugged. "The dog warden in

Clifford found him. He was a stray, so they brought him to us."

There were more throws and chases on the way back, until the girls and the dogs were safely in the Animal Magic yard.

"Do you fancy coming over after lunch and helping in the stables?" Eva asked.

Again, Annie nodded eagerly. "I'll see you in an hour."

"See you!" Eva replied, taking Holly inside to clean her paws on a towel and give her a nice dish of fresh, clean water.

Chapter Two

The afternoon turned out to be as busy as the morning. When Eva finally finished up at the computer in Reception, she was exhausted. She and Annie had mucked out the stables where they were housing two ponies, Peggy and Oliver, brought over by Cath Brown from Leebank Pony Sanctuary earlier that week. Then the girls had cleaned the litter trays in the cattery while Karl had stayed by the phone, leaving Jen and Heidi free to deal with two new admissions – a hamster called Maxwell, and Piper, a sleek white greyhound.

Meanwhile, Mark Harrison and Holly were out in his parcel van making deliveries. Eva had waved them off and smiled at Holly perched cheekily on the passenger seat next to her dad.

Now it had grown dark and all was quiet in the rescue centre. Jen had cycled home to Clifford. Annie had said goodbye and gone out with her mum and dad. And Karl and Heidi had gone over to the house to make tea, leaving Eva in charge of ordering more sweatshirts. "Animal Magic, Main Street, Okeham" – Eva typed the correct address on the order form, pressed Send, then turned off the computer. She was about to switch off the lights when the phone rang and she picked it up.

"Hello, this is Cath Brown," the voice said.

"Hi, Cath. This is Eva. Do you want to speak to Mum about Oliver and Peggy?"

"No, I just need you to pass on a message." The owner of the pony sanctuary sounded as if she was in a hurry.

"Go ahead," Eva said.

"I'm not sure, but I think I've just heard a kitten in distress."

"Whose kitten is it?" Eva asked, ready with pencil and paper. She planned to write down exactly what Cath told her.

"That's the problem – I'm not sure who it belongs to. I was out fixing the fence at the bottom of one of my fields and I heard it meowing inside a cottage down the lane from me — there were no lights on in the house or any other sign of life."

"You're sure the owners aren't out at the supermarket or something?" *Kitten*, Eva wrote. *Empty cottage.*

"I'm sure," Cath replied. "In fact, I know that the people who lived there moved out earlier this week. That's why I was surprised to hear a kitten crying and why I thought I should let you know. I'm afraid I have to go out now — a work thing — otherwise I'd have taken a look myself."

"Can you give me the address?" Eva asked, writing again as Cath spoke. *Willow Cottage, Leebank Lane.*

"Like I said, I might be wasting your time but I'd rather be safe than sorry."

A kitten crying inside a lonely cottage down a dark lane in the middle of winter – this certainly sounded worrying. "Thanks, Cath. I'll tell Mum." She hung up and ran across the yard to find Heidi.

Her mum listened carefully, then nodded. She reached for her jacket. "Come on, Eva, let's take a look!"

The drive to Leebank took twenty minutes along narrow roads that curved and rose and twisted and turned. Heidi's headlights drilled through the darkness, lighting up the stone walls to either side.

"Cath did warn me that there might be nothing wrong," Eva told her mum.

Heidi indicated, then turned down Leebank Lane. "Let's hope that's the case," she said quietly. "But meanwhile, we'll check anyway. There's Cath's place on the right – see the sign by the gate?"

Eva nodded. "She told me Willow Cottage is further down the lane. Slow down a bit, Mum, so I can take a proper look."

The car bumped and shuddered along the rough track. "I've never been down here before," Heidi admitted.

"There's something up ahead!" Eva pointed out. "A gate on the left and a farm track. Hang on, Mum – this could be it!"

Heidi braked and turned on to the track. Now their headlights revealed a low stone building and a sign on the gatepost that read "Willow Cottage".

"Come on!" Eager as ever, Eva jumped out. Heidi pulled a torch from her pocket and together they approached the house. "It looks deserted," Eva whispered.

Heidi listened then agreed. "I don't hear a kitten, do you? Maybe Cath made a mistake."

They listened again. A strong wind blew through the trees behind the house.

"Did you hear that?" Eva cried. Above the gusting wind she thought she heard a high, meowing cry. It was muffled and faint, but definitely there.

Heidi nodded. "Let's go round the back."

Eva ran ahead, stumbling against a rusty tractor parked at the side of the cottage, then picking her way over a pile of rubble.

"What a mess," Heidi muttered as she followed. She flashed her torch beam around the overgrown garden and the twisted willows growing by a stream.

"Over here, Mum – I've found the back door." Eva's eyes had grown used to the darkness and she could now make out an old wooden porch. Once more she stumbled in her hurry to reach the door.

Meow! Meow! There was no mistaking
it now – there was a kitten here in this
lonely place and it sounded as if the noise
was coming from the porch itself.

Eva found the door handle and pulled
hard. "It's locked!" she told Heidi.

Heidi shone the torch on the lock, then
rattled the handle. "We don't want to
break in if we can help it," she pointed out.

But the kitten's cries were growing louder and more pitiful. "We can't just leave it here with no one to look after it," Eva insisted.

Meow! The kitten must have heard their voices. It seemed to be begging them to rescue it.

"There's a window in the side of the porch," Heidi said. "It's not quite closed – let me see if I can slide my fingers in and lift the latch ... yes, that's it!"

Slowly the window opened and Heidi pushed aside a net curtain to aim her beam inside the porch.

Eva made out some cardboard boxes and a pile of yellowing newspapers sitting on top of a bench. Empty milk bottles were scattered across the stone floor.

Meow! Meow! Meow! The kitten's cries

were urgent, but still Heidi's torch beam couldn't locate the poor creature.

"Let me climb in!" Eva begged.

Her mum nodded, then gave her a leg-up. Eva squeezed through the window and jumped to the floor, knocking a milk bottle and making it roll as she landed. She peered under the bench, then into a plastic washing-up bowl resting on top.

A big pair of eyes stared back at her.

Eva gasped. "There you are!" she whispered. "Mum, give me the torch!" She took the light and shaded it with her hand to give her just enough light to see. "It's a little tabby kitten!" she reported. "There's nothing in this bowl except soggy newspaper – there are some unopened cans of food under the bench, but nothing

to drink. She must be *so* hungry and
thirsty!"

"Lift her out," Heidi decided. "See if
you can unlock the door from the inside.
Quickly, Eva, we need to get her back
to Animal Magic as soon as we can."

Chapter Three

"Well, what do you think?" Mark asked Heidi, while Karl and Eva stood back from the examination table. "It must have been pretty cold back there at the cottage. Did you rescue her in time?"

Please say yes! Eva crossed her fingers and held her breath. Her mum had tested the shivering kitten's heartbeat and thoroughly examined the inside of her mouth. Now they were waiting anxiously for Heidi's verdict.

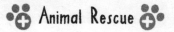

"She's a tough little thing," Heidi told them. "She seems surprisingly healthy after her ordeal."

"Cool!" Karl took a deep breath. "How old is she?"

"Six to eight weeks – scarcely weaned from her mother."

"So sweet," Eva murmured, venturing forward to stroke the rescue kitten. Back at Willow Cottage she'd lifted her out of the dirty plastic bowl and handed her through the porch window to Heidi. Together they'd taken her to the car, wrapped her in a blanket and put her safely in a pet carrier for the rough ride back to Okeham.

"She's lapped up the water from the dish so she won't need a rehydration drip," Heidi went on. "We'll start her off

on small amounts of kitten food – Karl,
can you fetch some from the cattery
store room? Thanks."

"Can I pick her up?" Eva asked.

"Yes. Snuggle her up, keep her nice
and warm."

So Eva picked up the tiny kitten.
She stroked between
her ears, noticing
the narrow stripes
running across her
head. "She looks
like a little tiger!"
she joked.

"She's definitely
loving your
cuddles." Mark
smiled as the kitten
began to purr.

"I don't suppose she's had many of those in her short life so far."

"I know. Someone moved out of the house and left her behind – how cruel is that!" Eva knew she shouldn't be surprised by how unkind people could be to their pets, but she always was.

"Well, she needs a name," Heidi said calmly. "And since you did the actual rescuing, it's your choice, Eva."

"Hmmm." Eva stroked the kitten's soft front paw and smiled at her little pink tongue as she opened her mouth to yawn. "How about Willow?"

"From Willow Cottage – very apt," her dad agreed. "It suits her."

"Meet Willow," Eva announced to Karl, as he came back with the kitten food and put it on the table.

Meow! The kitten smelled the food and wriggled free. Soon she was at the dish, tail in the air, head down, eating happily.

"Karl, make sure you take a really cute picture of Willow." It was early Sunday morning and Eva and Karl were preparing the kitten's details for the website.

"I always take cute pictures!" *Click-click* – Karl tapped the phone screen and looked at the result. He'd captured Willow with her head cocked to one side, staring straight at the lens. "See!" he grunted.

Meow! Willow cried.

"Aah, look – she wants to be cuddled!"

Eva picked the kitten up off the counter.

"Right, I'm off to upload the picture to the website," Karl said. "Then people can read the details and see how sweet she is."

As he dashed off, Eva stayed for a while with Animal Magic's newest resident. "That's our job," she murmured, putting her lips against Willow's soft, warm fur and explaining their next move. "We put your details on our website, and then we match the perfect pet with the perfect owner!"

"'Willow – how sweet is she!'" Eva read the words which Karl had written for the Animal Magic website out loud.

"'We hope this abandoned kitten won't be lonely for long!'"

"What do you think?" Karl asked Jen and Eva.

"That's perfect," Jen told him. "And with the picture to go with it, I'm sure it'll do the trick."

Karl nodded. "How much do you bet we won't keep Willow here for five minutes?"

Jen smiled as she went to open the front door, ready for business. "Yes, she's a little cutie. Hi, Cath – how are you?"

The pony sanctuary owner had been waiting in her car for the door to open. Now she breezed in, dressed in jeans and stable boots, bringing the smell of stables with her. "I'm fine, thanks. I was driving by and thought I'd pop in to check on Peggy and Oliver, and to catch up on the kitten situation."

"Come and take a look!" Eva invited Cath to check out Karl's website entry. "We called her Willow. Isn't she adorable?"

Cath smiled and nodded. "Heidi rang early this morning to say you'd rescued the poor little mite. She may have had a rough start in life, but by the look of things you plan to make up for it."

"Do you want to come to the cattery and see her?" Eva asked. Usually she was shy with the brisk, no-nonsense sanctuary owner but today Eva's excitement about the kitten overcame that. "Did Mum tell you where we found Willow?" she chatted on.

Cath nodded and followed Eva into the

cattery. "In the back porch – left there without a second thought about how she would survive," she replied. "It beats me how people can do these things, but you should see the awful condition of some of the ponies who come to me. Often nothing more than bags of bones... Oh, yes, I see what you mean!" Stopping beside Willow's cage, Cath leaned forward. "She really is pretty."

"Hello, Cath," Heidi said, coming out of the storeroom to greet their visitor. "I was just about to call you. I was thinking about Willow earlier and I wondered if the people who moved out of Willow Cottage left a forwarding address."

Eva frowned. Why did her mum even want to know?

Cath shook her head. "To tell the truth, I didn't even know their names. They were a youngish couple, but they only rented Willow Cottage and I hardly ever saw them in the six months they lived there."

"Cool," Eva said quickly. "Then we

don't need to try and trace them."

"Hold on," Heidi argued. "There's a chance that these people left Willow behind in the confusion of moving house and they've only just realized what they've done. In which case, they'll be back."

"No way!" Eva protested. She was eager to crack on and find a brilliant new home for Willow. "They definitely dumped her on purpose."

Heidi frowned. "We can't be certain, Eva. Cath, do you happen to know the landlord at Willow Cottage?"

"Yes. His name's Brian Verney – a sheep farmer on Briscoe Moor. Do you want me to give him a call?"

"Please," Heidi said. "I think we should be certain that the tenants can't be found before we post Willow's details on our website. Ask him if he has a forwarding address, and whether his tenants owned a tabby kitten."

"Will do," Cath agreed, smiling kindly at Eva and going out with Heidi to check on Peggy and Oliver.

Chapter Four

"We've got another new admission," Jen announced to Eva and Karl at the end of the Sunday morning session. "A stray dog without collar or identity chip. He's a mixture of all sorts, probably mostly Westie, picked up on Swallow Court after a phone call from Miss Eliot."

"Cool. Did Cath ring us?" Eva asked. She'd just come back from Annie's field where she'd been helping her friend pick out a stone wedged in Guinevere's shoe.

"Not yet," Jen told her, "unless she used Heidi's mobile number."

Eva dashed to the kennels where Heidi was settling in the new dog. "Mum, did you hear from Cath?" she asked.

"No," Heidi answered quietly. "Be patient, Eva."

How? Eva wondered, running back into Reception just in time to hear the phone ring. She darted to pick it up before Jen or Karl could get there. "Hello, this is Animal Magic Rescue Centre," she gabbled.

"Hi, Eva, this is Cath."

"Cool! I mean, hi, Cath. Have you got any news for us?"

"I finally got hold of Brian Verney," Cath said. "He's not happy. He told me the couple, who by the way are called Hines, did a moonlight flit from Willow Cottage."

"What does that mean exactly?" Eva frowned.

"They left without paying him the rent they owed, and without a forwarding address, so Brian has no way of getting the money out of them."

Eva nodded and gave Karl a quick thumbs up. "And does Mr Verney know if they had a kitten?"

"He said yes, they did, even though he has a no-pets rule for his tenants. They got one about a week before they did their flit. When he challenged them, they said they were only looking after the kitten for a friend, but Brian didn't altogether believe them. He said he was glad to get rid of them in the end."

Eva had put the phone on speaker for Jen and Karl to hear. They all grinned as Cath finished the story.

"Thanks, Cath, I'll tell Mum," Eva promised. She put down the phone and beamed at Karl. "Now we can get moving!" she cried. "Let's put Willow on the website and see how many calls we get in one afternoon!"

"We had seven calls about Willow, out of which there are three possible owners." Karl was almost as excited as Eva about their hopes for the abandoned kitten. He was chatting to their mum and dad over Sunday tea.

Mark turned to Eva. "What was wrong with the other four?"

"Two already own cats and Mum thinks Willow needs a home where she's the only one. One lives on a main road – too much traffic. The other woman said she'd call back in ten minutes but she never did."

"So what about the three who did make the list?" her dad asked, giving Eva a warning look as she let Holly sneak up to the table and beg for scraps.

"Bed, Holly!" Eva said sternly.

The puppy crept back to her basket by the stove.

Karl gave his dad the details. "Number one – Tom Ingleby at High Trees Farm. He wants a new farm cat to chase mice."

47

"And we like the Inglebys," Mark said.

"But it'd be a tough life for Willow," Eva pointed out. "She'd have to live in the barn, not in the house. She wouldn't really be a pet, would she?"

"So what about number two?" Mark asked Eva.

"Mrs Wilman," Karl cut in. "She lives on the far side of Clifford, which is a long way away, so Eva wasn't too keen on her."

Heidi smiled at her daughter. "I know you want to find a home for Willow close enough for you to go and visit, but that's not always possible."

Eva blushed. "Mrs Wilman did sound quite old," she pointed out. "She might not be able to cope with a new kitten."

"And number three?" her dad prompted.

"Jake and Julie Shannon," she answered quickly. "They're a young couple and they're new to Okeham."

"And where do they live?" Mark asked with a grin.

"In a lovely new house on Swallow Court, which is really quiet with hardly any traffic!" Eva said with a slow, satisfied sigh. "And it's just down the road from here!"

"The Shannons have arranged to come and see Willow at four o'clock today," Eva told Annie as they sat on the school bus on Monday afternoon. They sat side by side, looking out at the bleak grey fields on the way home to Okeham.

"They sound keen," Annie commented.

Eva nodded. All day at school she'd found it hard to concentrate, staring out of the window and dreaming about how much Willow would love living with the Shannons. They would give her a soft bed near a warm radiator and buy her lots of kitten toys. She would get the best food and probably wear a collar with a small bell, which would tinkle wherever she went. When Miss Jennings had read out the afternoon register, Eva hadn't even heard her name.

"Willow must be a special kitten," Annie sighed.

"What makes you say that?" Eva hadn't realized that she'd mentioned Willow's name to Annie at least

twenty times that day. "Willow likes
chicken flavour kitten food ... Willow
has stripes all over her body ...
Willow's meow is really cute...!"

Annie grinned. "I suppose it's because
you rescued her from Willow Cottage
yourself – that's what makes her special.
Anyway, can I come and see this mega
kitten before she leaves?"

Eva nodded. "Better be quick. Come
round before four o'clock."

"Eva, you haven't even met the
Shannons yet," Annie reminded her.

"I know, but..."

"But you've already made up your
mind. You want them to have Willow."
Annie laughed, getting up from her seat
and walking down the aisle as the bus
pulled up at their stop.

Annie was cuddling Willow in Reception when Julie and Jake Shannon walked in.

"I love her!" Annie told Eva, giving Willow a tickle under the chin.

Meow! The kitten lapped up the attention. She'd been at Animal Rescue for less than forty-eight hours but she'd already settled in beautifully.

"She's so friendly," Annie murmured as Willow purred.

"Is this her?" Julie Shannon asked Heidi, who'd greeted them from behind the desk. Julie was in her late twenties, with short fair hair and dressed in black leggings and a grey jacket. Her husband, Jake, stayed in the background, as if to let people know that having the kitten was mainly his wife's idea.

Reluctantly, Annie handed Willow to
Julie Shannon.

For Julie, it was love at first sight. "Oh, she's so pretty! I've never seen anything so cute and adorable!"

Once more, Willow accepted the cuddles. She peeped out from Julie's arms, her blue eyes gleaming, ears pricked.

"Isn't she lovely, Jake? Just like she was in the photo." Julie showed the kitten to her husband, who nodded and seemed happy if she was happy.

"Good, I'm glad you like her," Heidi said. "She's about two months old and she's had a hard time lately. She was abandoned, so she needs lots of TLC to make up for it."

"I find that so difficult to believe," Julie gasped, taking a tissue from her pocket to blow her nose. "How could anyone be so cruel?"

"At Animal Magic we identity-chip and vaccinate all our animals." Heidi went through the formal routine while Eva and Annie stood by. "Willow is perfectly healthy despite her ordeal and I'm sure she'll make a lovely pet."

"Are there a lot of people who want to adopt her?" Jake asked.

"We've certainly had plenty of interest," Heidi admitted.

But you're our first choice! Eva wanted to say. Instead she showed Annie her crossed fingers. "They seem really nice!" she whispered.

"So we do have to join the queue?" Jake frowned.

"Not necessarily," Heidi reassured him. "I'll ask you a few questions and if the situation seems satisfactory, we can make our decision on the spot."

Julie smiled and held Willow tight.

"So you live at number 22 Swallow Court?" Heidi checked.

Julie nodded. "Well away from Main Street, with open fields at the back of us."

"And have either of you owned pets before?"

"I haven't, but Jake has, haven't you?" Julie turned to her husband. "You had three cats at home when you lived with your parents."

"Yes, so I know the routines." Jake took over from Julie. "Apart from needing feeding, cats come and go pretty much as they please. And I guess I'll be the one who gets rid of the dead birds and mice."

"Willow won't chase birds," Julie
protested. "Look at her!"

Snuggled in Julie's arms, Willow
looked as if butter wouldn't melt in her
mouth.

"Oh yes she will, believe me," Heidi
smiled. "Dealing with dead offerings is
part of the cat-owning deal, I'm afraid."

In the background Eva grimaced.
Julie Shannon had just shown she didn't
know much about having a cat as a pet.
Would this worry her mum?

"Anyway, if there are any problems,
come back to Animal Magic – we're
only round the corner and we're always
ready to help," Heidi told the Shannons.

Good! Eva liked the sound of this. It
seemed as if her mum hadn't been put off.

And the more Eva saw of Julie and Jake,
the more sure she was that they were
Willow's perfect owners – young, lively
and loving.

Heidi smiled. "Do you have any
questions?" she asked them.

"No, I don't think so. Does this mean
we can have her?" Julie blew her nose
again and waited for Heidi's answer.

Please! Please! Eva begged silently.

Nestled in Julie's arms, Willow seemed
perfectly content.

"Yes," Heidi confirmed with a smile.
"We can provide you with kitten food
and a pet basket, and you can take
her with you now if you like. And let
me say we're very grateful to you for
offering Willow a home."

Chapter Five

It was the start of a very good week for Animal Magic.

On Tuesday the new sweatshirts arrived before Eva left for school, so she set them out in a rack in Reception next to the leaflets on animal care. Then she ran next door to deliver Annie's.

"They're very bright," Annie's mum, Linda, said doubtfully as she hobbled into the hall. She was still on crutches from an accident earlier in the month.

"And really warm," Eva told her. "You should have one for when you're better and mucking out Gwinnie and Merlin."

Linda nodded. "There's a thought. Yes, Eva, you're right – I'll need a medium size. Can you ask Heidi to put one aside for me?"

Eva skipped back home with the order.

"We make a profit of six pounds twenty pence every time we sell one." Karl had done the arithmetic. "At this rate, we'll raise loads of money."

Then on Tuesday evening, Jen managed to rehome Suzi, the worried black cat. "She's calmed down a lot since she came here," she told the middle-aged man who came to collect her. "In her last home, stress is what led to her over-grooming, so she needs peace and quiet – no children and no other pets."

"She'll suit me very well," Mr Howard told Jen. "I lead a quiet life now that I'm retired. And Suzi will be good company, I'm sure."

Eva was pleased to see Mr Howard go off with Suzi. She headed quickly for the computer to take her off the website. "Oops!" she said to Jen as she browsed the pages. "We left Becks on here by mistake. Shall I take her off as well?"

Jen nodded. "And take Piper off while you're at it, please."

Eva hesitated. "Didn't I just see Piper in the kennels?"

"Yes. But a couple came in to see him this morning and decided they'd like to have him. They've already given homes to two other greyhounds. They plan to pay us a series of visits with their other dogs so that Piper can get to know them gradually before they take him home."

"Good idea," Eva agreed. She took the picture of Piper off the site, then shut down the computer and went to help Heidi in the small animals unit.

"Come and see Bowie and Star," her mum invited. "They're a lovely pair of harlequins. Your dad brought them in this afternoon."

"Aah!" Eva smiled at the soft, cuddly rabbits hopping around their cage. "Where did Dad find them?"

"A girl at the supermarket checkout told him about them. Her neighbour wanted to sell them but couldn't find a buyer, so he was planning to set them free in the park. Better to bring them here than leave them in the park, so Mark got there just in time."

"My dad's a hero!" Eva grinned. "I want to tell him. Where is he now?"

"In the house cooking dinner."

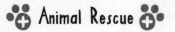

Eva scooted off to praise her dad, but
as she ran out of Reception she bumped
straight into Julie Shannon. "Hi!" she
said brightly. "How's Willow getting
on?"

"Fine."

Julie's answer seemed abrupt and Eva
noticed that her eyes seemed a bit red
and swollen, as if she'd been crying.
"Mum's in the small animals unit. Do
you want to speak to her?"

"Maybe you can help," Julie said with
a frown. "I hadn't realized that Willow
isn't house-trained yet. I was out at
work today and when I came home
I found she'd ignored the litter tray
and left wet patches all over our new
carpet."

"She's only young," Eva pointed out as

she led Julie into Reception. "It'll take her a while for her to learn to use the tray."

"I thought you might have some leaflets," Julie explained.

"We've got loads of fact sheets and advice," Eva said. She took four leaflets from the rack. "They tell you about the best type of cat litter, and keeping the tray clean – all that sort of stuff."

Julie nodded. "Thanks. I'll read them and follow their advice. Hopefully, tomorrow the carpets will stay dry."

As Eva showed Julie out and said goodbye, she had an uneasy feeling. "Otherwise, is everything OK?" she called after the visitor.

"Oh yes, absolutely fine," Julie said again, hurrying away.

Chapter Six

"Still no new home for you, Rocky,"
Eva said, as Karl brought the gentle
giant back from his walk. It was late
on Saturday afternoon – five days
since Willow had been adopted by the
Shannons – and everyone at Animal
Magic was enjoying another busy
weekend.

Rocky hung his head and patiently
allowed Karl to untangle his lead.

"Someone will want you soon," Eva

promised, patting his broad head.
"They just have to set eyes on you to
see what a gorgeous boy you are!"

"Right, that's me finished for the day,"
Jen announced, emerging from the
cattery and collecting the keys to her
bike lock from a drawer in Reception.
"Your mum's out in the stables,
administering wormers to Oliver and
Peggy. Tell her I'll see her tomorrow."

"Bye, Jen!" Eva and Karl called.

Karl took Rocky over to the kennels while Eva decided to take down all the out-of-date notices from the noticeboard. As she was busy doing this, there was a knock on the door. "Come in!" she called.

It was Jake Shannon who poked his head round the door. "Are you still open?" he asked.

"We're open twenty-four hours a day if it's an emergency," Heidi told him, appearing in the porch. "What can we do for you?"

"Well, it's not an emergency," Jake admitted. "It's more of an ongoing problem."

Uh-oh, Eva thought. *I bet Willow's still weeing everywhere.*

"To be honest, Julie's really stressing," Jake confessed, "and she's developed a really bad cold, which is making her feel terrible." He spoke quietly, in a shy voice, and his beige shirt and grey trousers seemed designed to make him fade into the background. "The fact is – Willow has started scratching the furniture when we're out. She's already made a mess of the table in the dining room and now she's started on the kitchen door."

Heidi listened then nodded. "That's common with young cats, I'm afraid. Have you tried buying her a specially designed scratching post?"

Jake sighed. "No, but I'll look for one on Monday morning. Will Willow grow out of scratching the furniture?"

"Some cats do," Heidi replied. "But it's

something cats do in the wild as a way
of exercising their claws and keeping
them sharp."

"So no guarantees?" Jake frowned.

"No, but try the scratching post. And
make sure Willow has some toys to play
with if she gets bored. That might take
her mind off scratching the furniture."

"OK, I'll do that," Jake promised,
taking this as his cue to leave.

"And I hope Julie gets better soon,"
Heidi added.

Jake nodded. "Thanks so much for
your help – bye!"

"Zero degrees." It was Sunday, and Jen
read the thermometer out in the porch

as she came into Reception, her face rosy from the bike ride into work. "It's a lovely clear day, but freezing!"

"No need to tell us," Karl groaned. "Eva and I took Rocky and Holly for a walk. We could see our breath, the air was so cold."

Mark grinned at them. "Stop complaining. I like this cold, crisp weather. With a bit of luck, we might even get snow."

"Hmm." Eva frowned. "I'd better remind Annie to make sure Gwinnie and Merlin are wearing their rugs tonight." She was close to the phone when it rang. "Hello, this is Animal Magic Rescue Centre."

"Hello, is that Eva? This is Miss Eliot from Swallow Court."

"Hi, Miss Eliot." Eva supposed that

the old lady wanted to check up on
the mare she'd once owned. "I was
just talking about Guinevere. Mum's
around, would you like to speak to her?"

"No thank you, dear. It's not Guinevere
that I'm ringing about." There was
a pause before Miss Eliot decided to
continue. "I don't want anyone to think
that I'm a busybody but I've just seen
something that I find rather worrying."

"To do with an animal?" Eva asked.
Otherwise, why would Miss Eliot call
Animal Magic?

"Yes. It's the tabby kitten at number
22."

"Willow!" Eva gasped.

Everyone in the room turned to Eva
and waited anxiously to hear what the
problem was.

"That's the one," Miss Eliot answered. "I can see the house from my front window and I'm always up early — before it gets light, as a matter of fact. Well, I was drawing back my curtains first thing this morning, and I saw the kitten sitting on the front doorstep, meowing to be let in."

"Oh!" Eva cried. "Does that mean Willow had been out all night?"

"I think so, dear. That's why I'm worried. The door was shut tight and there were no lights on. There was a deep frost everywhere."

"Out all night," Eva repeated. Willow was far too young to be out in such cold weather.

"She looked so lost and lonely," Miss Eliot concluded. "Honestly, my dear, it was pitiful to see."

"All right, let's take this slowly." As usual, Heidi wanted to think the problem through. "We mustn't jump to the wrong conclusion."

"What's to think about?" Karl wanted to know, while Eva frowned and bit her lip. "The Shannons locked Willow out of the house when it was freezing. Then they went to bed. How bad is that!"

"On the face of it, pretty bad," Heidi agreed. "But perhaps they didn't mean to do it. Mistakes happen, you know."

Jen agreed. "Or maybe Miss Eliot got it wrong. It's possible that either Julie or Jake were up early and had let Willow out for five minutes."

But Eva shook her head. "I don't think so. But it just doesn't make any sense. They both seemed so keen on having her … maybe they got tired of her weeing and scratching. She's so little – she could have frozen to death!" Eva looked at the evidence and rapidly changed her mind about the Shannons. Now she was certain that Animal Magic had sent Willow to the wrong home.

"It's true that Julie and Jake have been asking for advice," Jen acknowledged. "And Willow has been more work than they'd expected."

"Which proves that they're not used to owning a pet but that they're willing to learn," Heidi pointed out. "I don't think we can condemn them for making one mistake."

"A big mistake!" Karl insisted.

Heidi nodded. "But still, I would rather keep an eye on things and not do anything too hasty. If it turns out that the Shannons are deliberately leaving Willow out overnight, then I'm definitely prepared to have a word with them about how dangerous it could be."

Eva and Karl knew that their mum
had spoken her last word on the subject.
As Heidi returned to the morning's
business, they went to the kennels and
admitted how they felt.

"I know Mum wants to wait and see,"
Karl muttered, "but one more night
like last night could mean the end for
Willow!"

"Don't say that!" Eva cried. A picture
of the beautiful little kitten shivering
in the frosty night entered her head
and refused to go away. "Karl, we were
wrong about the Shannons. We made
a terrible mistake!" Eva felt guilty and
angry at the same time.

Leading Piper out of the kennels, Karl
agreed. "So what are we going to do?"

Eva thought hard. On the one hand, do nothing, as her mum had suggested. On the other, act in secret and save Willow before it was too late. "I'm going to Swallow Court," she decided.

"Just be careful," Karl warned as he set out with Piper. "Don't rush over there and do something stupid."

"OK, OK," she muttered. "But I don't care how I do it, I'm going to find out the truth!"

Chapter Seven

As Eva set off for Willow's new home, a light snow began to fall. She looked up at the dark grey sky, tied her scarf tightly under her chin, then strode on along Main Street.

"Hi, Eva." It was Karl's friend George Stevens who slowed her down. "Tell Karl to come to my house this afternoon. There's going to be loads more snow. We're making a massive snowman at the top of Earlswood Avenue."

More snow? Eva groaned as she turned into Swallow Court. Normally she'd have been enjoying the snow with George and his mates, but today she was more worried about the sub-zero temperature and the effect it would have on Willow. She walked quickly past Miss Eliot's house, crossed the street and headed for number 22.

No car parked outside the house, she thought as she approached the driveway. *So at least one of the Shannons must be out. No lights on, so they're probably both out.*

"Yoo-hoo, Eva!" Miss Eliot had come to her front door and was calling across the road. "Have you come about the kitten?"

Eva backtracked. "Hi, Miss Eliot. Yes, I was worried about Willow. I told Mum but she thinks we should wait a while before we do anything."

"Really?" The old lady sounded surprised. She bent down to pick up her elderly cat, Tigger, to stop him venturing out of the house. "Why did Heidi think that?"

Eva frowned and felt embarrassed. "Oh, it's not because she didn't believe you, Miss Eliot. But she wants to give the Shannons a second chance."

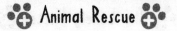

"She does?" Miss Eliot raised her eyebrows.

"Yes. Mum says it's possible they left Willow out by mistake."

"By mistake! Oh, I don't think so, dear." Gentle Miss Eliot suddenly sounded very firm. "If it had been a mistake, they wouldn't have done it again."

"Again?" It was Eva's turn to sound surprised as she looked anxiously across at number 22.

"And so soon. Listen, my dear, I've been keeping a close eye on that house ever since I called you. And guess what – that young couple didn't open the door to let the kitten in until after breakfast. I was relieved, of course. But then, no sooner did they let her into the warmth than they turned her out again."

"What do you mean?" Eva asked.

Miss Eliot looked straight at her. "They went out in the car at about ten o'clock. But before they drove off, they made sure to shoo the kitten out into the front garden and lock the door on her."

"Here, Willow!" Eva searched amongst the frozen flower beds in the Shannons' front garden. Now she didn't care what anyone said – after what Miss Eliot had just told her, she knew she had to rescue the kitten.

She called again, then spotted tiny, faint paw prints in the snow. They led from the front doorstep around the side of the house.

Quickly, Eva followed them.
"Willow!" she called again, scared
that the fast-falling snow would cover
up the only clue the kitten had left.
She reached the back garden and took
in the stack of cardboard packaging
leaning against the fence. "Willow,
where are you?" she called softly.

By now the paw prints had almost
disappeared under fresh snow. Eva
could just make out that they were
heading for the stack of cardboard, so
she made her way there, gently lifting
the flattened boxes to peer behind
them.

Meow! With a loud terrified cry, Willow
shot out from behind the sheets of
cardboard.

"Willow, it's me – Eva!"

Meow! Meow! The frightened kitten cowered on the back doorstep.

Eva was down on her knees, trying to coax Willow to come to her when the Shannons' car returned. She heard the engine stop and doors open and then slam. There wasn't enough time for her to find a hiding place. *How am I going to explain this?* she thought, picturing the Shannons' faces when they discovered her in their snowy back garden.

She froze, listening to the key turning in the front door, feeling the soft snowflakes land on her cold forehead and cheeks. After a short while, the back door opened.

"Willow, here's your breakfast!" Jake Shannon called. He rattled a dish of dry cat food to tempt the kitten back into

the house. Then he saw Eva. "Blimey!"
he muttered. "Hey Julie, there's an
intruder in our back garden!"

Chapter Eight

In spite of the cold, Eva felt her face flush bright red as she stood in Jake and Julie Shannon's kitchen watching Willow eat.

The moment the kitten had heard Jake rattle the dish, she'd shot between his legs into the house. Julie had joined her husband at the kitchen door and asked Eva to come in and explain.

"I was worried about Willow," Eva stammered. "She's too little to be out in the snow, so I was trying to catch her before she froze."

Julie frowned. "How did you know she was outside?"

Don't mention Miss Eliot! Eva knew she mustn't involve the old lady. "I was just passing and I heard meowing."

"We'd only driven to the chemist's." Julie was cross. "We weren't out long. Willow would have been quite all right," she sniffled, blowing her nose.

Eva nodded unhappily. "I'm sorry."

"That's OK. Don't be too hard on Eva," Jake told Julie. "She wasn't to know how soon we'd be back. And she was obviously worried about Willow."

"Well, she doesn't need to be. *We're* her owners now."

"Sorry." Eva knew that if Julie was

cross enough to call Heidi, she'd be in big trouble back home.

"Time for you to take that medicine and put your feet up," Jake suggested to his wife after an awkward silence. "And time for you to go, Eva." He led her down the hall towards the front door.

"I realize we're not doing very well with Willow," he confided quietly as she stepped out on to the drive. "It's much more difficult than we expected. Moving house is a stressful time, plus Julie is a perfectionist. She hates mess. And to cap it all, she hasn't been very well."

Eva nodded slowly. *So why get a pet?* she wondered. *Pets equal stray hairs and muddy feet. Pets are messy, full stop.*

"We'll try harder from now on, I promise," Jake said.

She wanted to believe him. "And you won't leave her out again?"

"No," he said, before firmly closing the door.

So Eva went home and worried all day. She worried about Willow all that evening, and after she went to bed she lay awake, worrying.

"Where are you now, Willow?" she whispered, staring out of her bedroom window at the starlit sky.

She thought back over the day. By lunchtime the snow clouds had cleared and Karl had spent the afternoon with George, building the giant snowman at the top of Earlswood Avenue. Eva had stayed at home and missed all the fun.

"Are you all right?" her dad had asked. "Or is something bothering you?"

"I'm fine," Eva had lied.

But now she couldn't sleep. She sat up in bed, pulled back the curtains and gazed out of the window. She saw the pale full moon shining on a white world of snow-covered hills and a sleeping village. And she hoped with all her heart that Willow wasn't out in the white wilderness, but safely snuggled up in a soft bed in the warm kitchen of 22 Swallow Court.

Chapter Nine

At school the next day, Eva tried hard to concentrate. But every time her teacher told her to do something, her mind drifted off to the problem of Willow.

At least it's not snowing, she told herself, looking out at a clear blue sky.

"Eva, did you hear me?" Miss Jennings asked from the front of the class. "I asked you to take this message to the school secretary's office."

It's sunny but it's still freezing, she thought,

standing out in the playground with Annie during lunch break.

"Hello? Do you want me to help with the ponies when we get home?" Annie asked. "Honestly, Eva, I've said it three times. What's wrong with you today?"

The day dragged until at last Eva sat on the bus, still in a world of her own.

"So tell me!" Annie insisted.

"It's Willow," Eva confessed. The story tumbled out. "New home ... the Shannons ... out all night ... a terrible mistake!"

Annie listened carefully. "I get it," she muttered. "You think that if you wait too long before your mum decides to step in, it might be too late."

Eva gulped then nodded. "But I messed up yesterday. Jake and Julie caught me trespassing in their back garden. I'm scared they'll tell Mum."

"And she'd be really cross." Annie understood the problem. She thought for a while. "Maybe we should go undercover?"

"You mean like spies, rescuing Willow in secret?" Eva's glum face began to light up. "You think we should kidnap her?"

"Catnap!" Annie said. The bus drew into Okeham and the village kids filed off. "We could go to Swallow Court and start right now."

Without stopping to think, Eva agreed and she and Annie clambered off the bus. "If the house is empty and Willow has been left outside all day, it means that Jake didn't keep his promise," she said. "Which means we have to do something!"

"Catnap her," Annie said again. "Act casual, Eva, as if we're just coming down here for a stroll."

They paused outside Miss Eliot's house, pretending to gossip but really taking a sneaky look at number 22. There was no sign of life, until all of a sudden a car turned off Main Street into the cul-de-sac.

"It's the Shannons' car! Quick, follow me," Eva hissed, bolting through Miss Eliot's gate and knocking at her door.

The old lady soon appeared. "Eva, Annie, how nice to see you!" she exclaimed. "Come in out of the cold."

"Good thinking," Annie muttered to Eva, as, five minutes later, they sat in Miss Eliot's sitting room with orange juice and biscuits. From here they'd had a good view of Julie Shannon getting out of her car and going into the house.

Eva nodded. "Let's stay as long as we can," she mumbled.

Miss Eliot's cat, Tigger, rubbed against her legs, then jumped on to her lap.

"Is there any more news about the kitten?" Miss Eliot asked, noticing that Eva was studying the goings-on at number 22.

"Not today," Eva replied, seeing Julie come out to unload some shopping from the car. There was no sign of Willow. Another five minutes went by before the front door flew open again. This time Julie appeared carrying the little kitten at arm's length. Willow hung like a scrap of fur from her hands, legs dangling.

Eva jumped up, sending Tigger sliding to the floor. "It's happening again!"

Miss Eliot, Annie and Eva rushed to the window to see Julie dump Willow on the doorstep and close the door, leaving her meowing to be let back in.

"Poor thing!" Miss Eliot murmured
with a shake of her head. "I'd adopt her
myself, but Tigger wouldn't like it. He's
been an only cat for far too long."

"Watch out, here comes Mr Shannon!"
Annie warned as she spotted Jake

walking towards the house, briefcase in
hand.

He immediately spotted Willow,
and bent down to stroke the top of her
head. Then he scooped her up and took
her inside. But a few moments later he
reappeared with a cat basket.

"What's he doing now?" Eva
demanded, so mad that she was ready
to rush out and confront Jake Shannon.

Miss Eliot tried to calm her. "Wait.
Now Mrs Shannon has joined them. Her
eyes are red. She looks upset. Oh dear!"

Jake and Julie seemed to be arguing.
Jake had Willow in the basket and was
opening the car door. Julie was in the
driving seat, wiping her eyes.

"He's getting in – they're driving
away!" Annie cried.

"Where to? What are they doing?" Eva couldn't wait any longer. She rushed to Miss Eliot's front door and ran into the garden – just in time to see Julie reverse out of their drive and pull away.

Chapter Ten

"Oh no, what now?" Eva felt rooted to the spot. In her mind's eye she saw Jake and Julie Shannon driving out of the village into the countryside, choosing a deserted place and stopping the car to dump their unwanted kitten.

"This is awful," Annie groaned as she joined Eva on the pavement. "If only we had a car, we could follow them."

Miss Eliot had stopped to put on her coat. Now she came out of the house, shaking her head.

Annie turned to Eva, flustered. "What do we do?"

"We have to get back to Animal Magic," Eva decided. "I'll be able to look up the Shannons' mobile phone number there. Then Jen or Mum can try to call them."

So the girls said goodbye to Miss Eliot and sprinted to Main Street. "Please don't let us be too late!" Eva gasped as she and Annie ran on until they came to the rescue centre. She was so worried that at first she didn't notice the car parked in the yard.

"Eva, wait!" Annie grabbed hold of her arm and pointed to the Shannons' car. "They didn't drive off with Willow – they brought her back here!"

In Reception, Heidi and Jen listened patiently to Julie's tearful account.

"I'm so sorry," she wept. "I've brought Willow back. I love her dearly but I can't keep her."

Eva and Annie were quiet as they came through the door. Jake Shannon glanced over his shoulder and gave them an apologetic smile.

"I'm so, so sorry, Willow!" Julie cried.

"And in spite of what you might think, it hasn't got anything to do with her weeing on the carpets and scratching the furniture." Jake stood up for Julie.

"It turns out that I have a severe cat allergy," Julie explained through her tears. "I got up this morning and I could hardly breathe. My eyes were streaming. So I went to see my GP. He confirmed that I didn't have a cold but was having a serious allergic reaction to Willow."

Jake put his arm around his wife and took up the explanation. "Obviously we didn't want to leave Willow outside on Saturday but Julie was finding it so hard to breathe – it was as if she was having an asthma attack – and we both panicked. But then yesterday we got some tablets at the chemist's and she felt a bit better. She wanted to try again. Then this morning she felt even worse and decided to see the doctor. Her allergy is very acute and he advised us not to keep Willow."

I never expected this! Eva thought, going up to the counter and lifting Willow out of the cat basket. The kitten was shaking. "Hush!" Eva whispered.

"Take Willow into the cattery," Heidi told her. She turned back to Julie. "Don't feel bad," she said kindly. "You weren't to know you were allergic."

"Julie's never lived in a house where there's been a cat before," Jake explained.

"You did the right thing," Heidi said. "And don't worry about Willow."

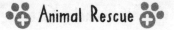

Julie dried her tears. "She'll go to a good home?"

Heidi nodded. "Of course. And until that special person finds her, we'll take good care of her here."

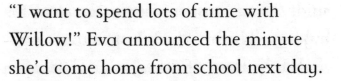

"I want to spend lots of time with Willow!" Eva announced the minute she'd come home from school next day.

After she'd dropped off her school bag in the house, said hi to Holly and played with her for ten minutes, she'd hurried to the cattery.

Jen agreed that the lonely kitten needed plenty of attention. "At the moment she's a bit wary of people – not surprising after what she's been through."

"I'll take her to Reception," Eva decided. "It'll do her good to be around people."

So she took Willow from her cage and carried her to the busy reception area, where Cath Brown happened to have called in for a chat with Heidi and Karl.

"I saw Rocky on your website," Cath said. "I was browsing – getting ideas for my own website which I plan to set up – and the picture of Rocky hit me between the eyes. He's a handsome chap."

Karl nodded. "Rocky's brilliant."

"He might be what I need," Cath admitted. "I'm isolated out at Leebank. I could do with a good guard dog."

Eva tickled Willow's tummy. "You hear that? If Rocky goes with Cath, it'll be cool."

"Listen, Cath." Heidi made a suggestion. "I know it's dark but would you like Karl to take you and Rocky along Main Street, so you can get a look at how good he is on the lead?"

Quickly agreeing, Cath waited for Karl to bring Rocky from the kennels. "By the way," she told Eva as she watched her play with Willow. "Seeing the kitten reminds me – I was down in my field this morning finishing off the repairs to my fence, when I saw someone in the garden at Willow Cottage. I thought it must be a new tenant, but when I bumped into Brian Verney, he told me he hasn't found anyone for the cottage yet. So I'm still on my own down the lane, except for the ponies, of course."

"And maybe Rocky!" Eva smiled at Cath as Karl came back with a pleased-looking dog. "He loves walks," Eva explained to Willow as Rocky went off with Cath and Karl. "And I think Cath likes him, so fingers crossed…"

It was only later, when she was in bed, that Eva thought again about what Cath had mentioned.

So who was in the garden at Willow Cottage? she wondered. *Why would anybody be snooping around unless they wanted to rent the place?*

The clock ticked on her bedside table and a bright moon shone through the gap in her curtains.

Maybe the old tenants came back for Willow, she thought. *But then again, why would they? The Hineses definitely didn't want her, or else they wouldn't have dumped her in the porch. Anyway, stop thinking about it and go to sleep!*

But the clock ticked and Eva stayed awake.

Wait a sec – what did Mr Verney tell Cath

about his no-cats rule? He said he thought the Hineses had lied and told him they were looking after Willow for a friend. But what if they weren't lying? What if they were telling the truth?

Eva sat up in bed. "Willow's owner came back to collect her!" she breathed. "But when she got to Willow Cottage it was empty and Willow had gone!"

Chapter Eleven

"Tom Ingleby is still keen on having Willow up at High Trees Farm," Mark told Eva when she came home from school the next day. "He saw her back on the website and says he'll pop in tomorrow teatime."

All day Eva had been in a fever of what-ifs and buts. *What if Willow's owner really did come back? But maybe they're not a good owner. Either way, I have to find out.* Eva had been in such a hurry to get back

home that she'd left the books she needed
for her homework in her school locker.

"Dad, can we ask Mr Ingleby to wait a
while?" she asked now.

Mark gave his daughter a quizzical
look. "Why?" he asked.

"I want to call Mr Verney," she said,
deliberately keeping it vague.

Her dad thought for a while, then
smiled. "More detective work? OK, Eva,
go ahead. You've got twenty-four hours."

With fumbling fingers, Eva dialled the
farmer's number. "Hello, Mr Verney? This
is Eva Harrison from Animal Magic…"

"Well?" Eva's dad asked when she came
off the phone. He'd watched her face

change from a frown to a smile and back again. "Was it good news, or not?"

"Mr Verney said that a woman did ring him this morning to ask what had happened to the Hineses."

"The old tenants at Willow Cottage?"

Eva nodded. "Mr Verney told her that they'd gone without leaving a forwarding address. But, Dad, I think the woman might be Willow's real owner!" And she raced on and explained her brainwave from the night before.

"Slow down!" Mark begged. "Take me back to the conversation you just had with Brian Verney. Did this mystery woman leave a name?"

Eva sighed and shook her head. "That's the problem," she confessed.

"She talked to Mr Verney, then hung up without telling him who she was."

"It's so sad," Eva murmured to Willow when she went to the cattery to take her out of her cage. She pulled up a stool and sat the kitten on her lap. "There's a woman out there and I'm sure she's looking for you, but there's no way I can find out who she is!"

Willow snuggled against Eva's warm sweatshirt. She looked up at Eva with her sweet face.

"So even if she is your real owner, you'll probably go to live with the Inglebys," Eva went on. "They're very nice, I promise, but you'll have to chase

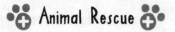

mice and work hard when you grow
up."

Meow! Willow sat on her haunches
and reached up to paw the gold logo on
Eva's sweatshirt.

Suddenly, Karl burst into the cattery.
"Guess what!" he said. "Cath just rang
to say she's been thinking about it all
day and she's finally decided to take
Rocky. She's on her way right now."

"Brilliant!" Scooping up Willow, Eva
rushed to Reception, where she waited
eagerly with Heidi for Cath to arrive.

Karl soon reappeared with an excited
Rocky, who wagged his long tail and
padded on his big paws around the
waiting area.

At last Cath's Land Rover drew up in
the yard. "Here she is – and she's got

someone with her," Karl reported from the porch. He held the door open for Cath and her companion.

"Hey, Rocky – that's my boy!" Cath smiled as he recognized her from the previous day. Rocky hurried to greet her with a low woof and an extra big wag of his tail. "Eva, Heidi, Karl – this is Lucy and I think you'll be very pleased to meet her!"

Eva smiled at the young stranger who stood in the doorway. The dark-haired woman wore a sloppy, patterned jumper, jeans and fur-lined boots. At first Eva thought the visitor was staring at her, but then she realized that Lucy's gaze was fixed on Willow.

"Lucy knocked on my door just as I was leaving to come here," Cath explained as she stroked Rocky and made a fuss of him. "Over to you, Lucy," she said with a smile.

"I've been handing out these leaflets at all the houses around Leebank." The woman showed them a pile of printed notices.

Eva took one and read it. "Lost – tabby kitten, eight weeks old. £50 reward." She read it again, to make sure. "You're Willow's owner!" she cried.

Lucy Marriott's story made perfect sense.

"My dad fell ill. He lives in Scotland and I had to go and look after him," she told Eva, Heidi and Karl. "It was very sudden. I'd just moved into the Okeham area – Danny and Polly Hines were the only people I'd met and they agreed to take care of my new kitten at the last minute. I'd no idea they were about to do a runner. As soon as Dad was well enough for me to leave, I phoned Polly and she said that they'd had to leave Willow Cottage in a big hurry. She told me they'd left Pixie in the back porch with plenty of food and water. But when I came back to collect her, she'd disappeared. And I've been trying to find her ever since."

"Pixie — is that Willow's real name?" It felt strange to Eva to hand the kitten over to Lucy. She had a lump in her throat and tried hard not to let her feelings show.

"Yes. I'd only had her for a few days before I left." Lucy smiled as she took Willow. "I like the name 'Willow', though. Perhaps I could change it."

"That would be nice, for Eva's sake," Cath said. "Eva's the one who saved Willow's life." And she told Lucy the full story. "There was no food in the dish and the temperature outside was pretty low. But Eva never gives up on an animal in trouble," she concluded.

"Then I'll definitely call her Willow

as a way of saying thank you!" Lucy
promised, with a warm smile at Eva.
"Plus, I'll donate the fifty pounds
reward to Animal Magic. And I'll leave
you my address so you can come and
visit her any time you like."

Willow and Lucy Marriott had left the
rescue centre in Cath's car. The last
glimpse Eva had of the kitten was of
her snuggled in a blanket inside a pet
carrier that Heidi had provided. She
looked warm and happy – glad to be
going home at last.

"Bye, Rocky," Karl murmured as
Cath let him jump up into the back
of her Land Rover.

"Bye, Willow," Eva sighed.

She, Karl and Heidi had been joined by Mark and Holly. Together they watched the red lights on the back of Cath's car disappear down Main Street.

"Well done, everyone," Heidi said as they stood in the dimly lit yard.

"Yes," Mark agreed. "It was great detective work on Eva's part. And thank heavens Lucy turned up when she did! But we'll have to let poor Tom Ingleby know…"

Karl sighed, then picked up a stick and threw it. "Fetch!" he told Holly.

The puppy ran and neatly caught the stick. Everyone clapped.

"Well caught, Holly!" Eva cried. "We'll teach you lots of new tricks, then enter you into competitions and train you to be the best sheepdog in the country, if not the whole world!"

Mark laughed, putting his arm around Eva's shoulder. "And if Eva's teaching you, you probably will be!"

Have you read...

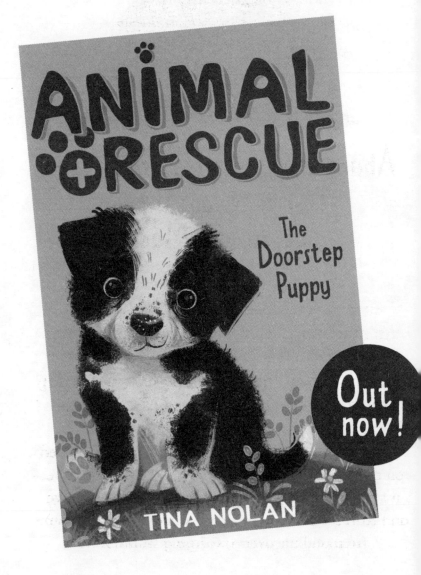

ANIMAL RESCUE

The Doorstep Puppy

Out now!

TINA NOLAN

Abandoned ... lost ... neglected?
There's always a home
at Animal Magic!

In a perfect world there'd be no need for
Animal Magic. But Eva and Karl Harrison,
who live at the rescue centre with their
parents, know that life isn't perfect. Every day
there's a new arrival in need of their help!

When Holly, a gorgeous Border collie, is abandoned
on the doorstep of Animal Magic on Christmas Eve,
it's up to the team to nurse her back to health. Eva
and Karl set out to investigate where Holly has come
from and uncover a worrying situation...

Have you read...

ANIMAL RESCUE

The Sad Pony

Out now!

TINA NOLAN

Abandoned ... lost ... neglected?
There's always a home
at Animal Magic!

In a perfect world there'd be no need for
Animal Magic. But Eva and Karl Harrison,
who live at the rescue centre with their
parents, know that life isn't perfect. Every day
there's a new arrival in need of their help!

When Linda Brooks breaks her leg, she's no longer
able to look after Rosie, her lively Shetland pony.
Animal Magic agree to take in Rosie but it's not
easy finding her a perfect new home. Will one
of Eva's brilliant ideas save the day?

Collect them all!

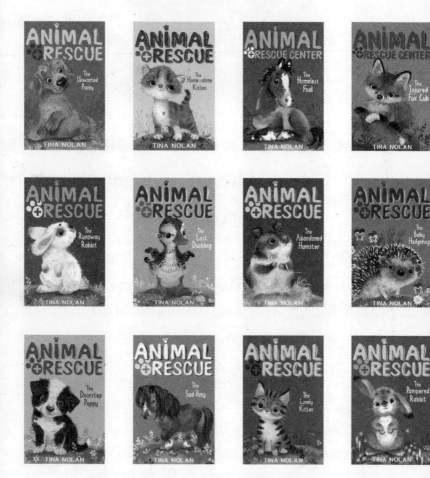